MEESHA MAKES FRIENDS

TOM PERCIVAL

BLOOMSBURY
CHILDREN'S BOOKS
LONDON OXFORD NEW YORK NEW DELHI SYDNEY

Meesha LOVED
making things.

She could make pictures
out of numbers . . .

and pictures
out of sounds.

Sometimes she made
pictures out of *both*.

But there was one thing that Meesha
found hard to make . . .

friends.

Everybody else seemed to find it easy. But not Meesha.

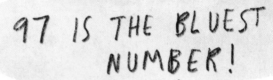

When she tried, she didn't know what to do, what to say or *when* to say it.

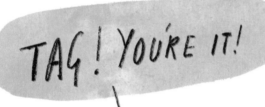

For Meesha, making friends was so difficult
that she wondered if she would *ever*
be able to do it.

Then, one evening, Meesha had an idea.

She got out her paints, her pencils
and all her other tools.

Then she started to
cut and stick and
glue and sew.

Soon she had made a
whole *group* of really fun friends.

Friends that were
easy to be around.

Friends that she could take with her
wherever she went.

Admittedly, Meesha's new friends
weren't very good at tennis . . .

or football . . .

or catch.

But Meesha felt comfortable with them,
and *that* was what mattered.

One day, Meesha's mum
said they were going
to a party.

She *said* there would be
lots of nice people there.

She *said* it would be fun.

Meesha wasn't
so sure.

The party was noisy, chaotic and unpredictable.
Everyone else was playing together . . .

and Meesha just *couldn't*
find a way to join in.

She ran off to find a quiet corner
where she could make her
own friends.

Meesha sat happily for a while until
she realised that something didn't feel right.

A boy was watching her.

"Hi, I'm Josh. Can I see
what you're making?"

For a while Meesha said nothing.

But then she took a deep breath
and showed him her friends.

"Wow!" gasped Josh. "They're amazing!
Can you show me how to make one?"

Meesha was worried.

What if he got it all wrong?
What if he spoiled everything?

But Josh didn't *look* like he would
try to spoil things. So . . .

Meesha showed him what to do.

And do you know what? Josh *didn't* get it all wrong and he didn't spoil anything either.

In fact, now that she was making things
with someone else . . .

it was *even* better!

Soon Meesha *and* Josh had built
a whole town for their friends
to live in – *together*.

"Let's go and show the others!" said Josh.

Meesha wasn't sure.

But Josh's smile made her feel that
it would all be OK.

AND IT WAS!

For the first time *ever* Meesha knew
exactly what to say *and* what to do.

And that was how the friends
that Meesha made . . .

helped Meesha make
friends.